Leapfrog
Rhyme
Time

Pets on Parade

by Jillian Powell

Illustrated by Gwyneth Williamson

W
FRANKLIN WATTS
LONDON•SYDNEY

It was "Bring Your
Pet to School" day.
Most children brought a pet.

There were dogs and cats and rabbits,

and a cheeky marmoset.

Sam had brought
his hamster.

It was running
round its wheel.

May had brought
her kitten.

It thought the hamster
was a meal!

Dan had eight
stick insects.

They looked
like lots of sticks.

But two got out along
the way ...

then there were only six!

Jenny had a tiny mouse.

She kept it in her pocket.

But when the mouse
saw all the cats,

it shot off like a rocket.

Toby had a ferret.

He had taught it
how to roll.

But when the ferret saw
the mouse ...

both vanished
down a hole!

Then in came Ricky Brown.

He was carrying a box.

What could be inside it?

A tortoise or a fox?

And everyone began
to scream as Ricky
let it out ...

the biggest snake
they'd ever seen was
slithering about!

Dogs were playing.

Cats were chasing.

They were making
such a noise.

Then Miss Brett stood up
and shouted,

30

"Take your pets home, girls and boys!"

Leapfrog Rhyme Time has been specially designed to fit the requirements of the Literacy Framework. It offers real books for beginner readers by top authors and illustrators.

Other Leapfrog titles also available:

Leapfrog Fairy Tales

A selection of favourite fairy tales, simply retold.

Leapfrog

Fun, original stories by top authors and illustrators.

For more details go to:

www.franklinwatts.co.uk

* hardback